A Splash of Short Stories Large Print

Dawn Knox

Copyright

A Record of this Publication is available from the British Library.

ISBN: 9798336231403

This edition is published by Affairs of the Heart

Editing – Wendy Ogilvie Editorial Services

To Mum and Dad

Thank you for believing in me

Contents

Foreword

I would like to thank Gill James from Chapeltown Books for introducing me to flash fiction. I first saw stories written in 100 words on her e-Zine CafeLit, and I was intrigued, although I wasn't convinced I'd be able to write one. However, my first drabble, 'The Betrayal', was published by Gill on the CafeLit site in 2014.

Since then, I've often turned to writing flash fiction to amuse myself, to record random observations and – particularly at those sad times in my life – to cope when I felt my heart was breaking.

The drabbles in this collection have been written during the last few years. Some reflect my interest in fractured fairytales, others record my observations during the Covid lockdown, and still others voice my thoughts at the sad loss of my parents. So, you can see, they range from humorous to heartfelt.

Recently, I've challenged myself to write a drabble a week which I've submitted to Friday Flash Fiction.

Drabbles published by CafeLit have been marked with one asterisk and those published by Friday Flash Fiction are marked with two.

Whatever your mood, I hope you find something that appeals to you.

CafeLit –

Friday Flash Fiction –

Chapter 1
The New Bed and Breakfast

**

He studied his wife's face and then his son's. The family was sitting at the kitchen table, and the atmosphere was gloomy.

"I'm not sure this experiment is working," he said, and his son nodded vehemently.

"Let's not be hasty, love," his wife said. "We agreed to give it a few weeks. It's only been a couple of days."

"But setting up a Bed and Breakfast was supposed to make life easier."

"We've only had one guest so far, love. Others might be less of a problem."

The door opened and Goldilocks strode in. "I have a complaint," she said.

Chapter 2
A Word with the Landlord

*

"Well, I can only tell you what I've seen, and the evidence looks pretty damning to me. When they signed the lease, they claimed they were a family of three. But I know for a fact there are four people living in that house. The only explanation is that they're contravening their contract and are sub-letting."

"Could they have had a baby?"

"No, the fourth person is an adult. And from what I've seen, she's definitely at home. She eats there and sleeps there. And anyway, trust me, Mother Bear did not give birth to a girl with blonde hair."

Chapter 3
A Mother's Woes

**

She wondered if her only son, Jack, was unlucky or stupid.

She'd eventually forgiven him for exchanging their cow for a packet of seeds. After furiously throwing them all into the garden, they'd grown into giant beanstalks which she'd sold on eBay. All except one, which had been commandeered by a giant. A very loud giant. And he'd refused to move out.

Jack had promised to solve the problem by making a dreadful racket as he practised on his new trumpet.

She'd been impressed until the giant had invited Jack to a jamming session and joined in on his drums.

Chapter 4
As Rare As...

"Ma! I'm home."

"Jack! You're late! I expected you hours ago. Tell me what happened."

"Don't fret, Ma! I found the man, and he agreed to give me a refund."

"I should think so, too. A fine cow is worth far more than a handful of beans."

"I told you he was reasonable."

"So, where's the cow?"

"He said he'd deliver it tomorrow. But it's not a cow. I negotiated a better deal than that."

"What's better than a cow?"

"Look, here's a photo. I picked it from his catalogue."

"Numptie! What are we going to do with a unicorn?"

Chapter 5
Oil's Well That Ends Well

*

"You've paid for what, Jack? An oil well?"

"Yes! It's so exciting! The Goblin's going to drill a well for us and take care of the extraction. We'll make a fortune."

"Goblin! You trusted that grasping, deceitful Goblin?"

"Don't be like that, Ma. He's done tests that show the oil's under our lawn."

"And how much have you paid him?"

"Only fifty pieces of gold."

Jack's mother's knees buckled. She sat at the kitchen table, her head in her hands.

“Ma, trust me! I’ve got guarantees. The Goblin promises we’re going to produce the finest olive oil in the country.”

Chapter 6
The Sleeping Princess

*

"Kiss her? What d'you mean, kiss her? She's asleep. I'm not going to touch her! What on earth are you thinking?"

"But, Highness, you're the prince. She's the sleeping princess. You've got to kiss her, or she won't wake up and she's already been asleep for a hundred years. She needs a break."

"Forget it, buster! The last time I kissed a sleeping princess, it took weeks for the bruises to go down. And after that piercing scream, my eardrums have never been the same."

"But..."

"No, forget it. She looks pretty peaceful to me. Let's leave her to it."

Chapter 7
A Good Insurance Policy

"I understand your frustration, madam, but since you've contravened the T&Cs of your Forest Insurance Company policy, there'll be no payment.

"First, your property was unsecured. Second, you invited a wolf into your house.

"Yes, I understand the perpetrator was posing as your granddaughter. Nevertheless, Forest Insurance cannot be held responsible for the ensuing fracas.

"However, before I go, if you require advice about insuring your hands against damage, please let me know. Yes, I'm fully aware you have a black belt in karate. One poleaxed wolf says it all. But a policy insuring those hands would be most advisable..."

Chapter 8
Let Them Eat Cake

*

"Come on Sis, eat up! This cake's delicious."

"Hansel, you're such a numpty! Don't you see she's trying to fatten us up to go in a pie?"

"But I'm starving!"

"Excuse me!" A robin chirped from the window next to the children's cage. "Do you have any more of those delicious crumbs you left outside, please?"

"The stupid bird's eaten the crumb trail you dropped, Gretel! If we escape, we'll never find our way home!"

"Watch and learn," said Gretel. "Robin, if you bring me the keys from the table and show us home, there's a whole slice for you."

Chapter 9
Embracing New Technology

*

"It's no good," said the witch with a cackle. "You won't get a signal here in the forest."

"Wrong!" said Gretel, holding up her mobile phone.

"She's sent Dad a text. He'll be here shortly," said Hansel.

"Bah! I'm starving and you looked so juicy!" said the witch, collapsing on her chair. "When my blood sugar drops, I get really grumpy."

"Well, what do you fancy?" asked Gretel.

The witch drooled as she listed things she'd like to eat, "Sausages, custard, doughnuts, chips..."

"Done," said Gretel, her fingers flying over her phone. "Tescado should deliver your order within the hour."

Chapter 10
An Important Customer

*

Typical. The first time anyone of quality has ever come into my shop and she's asking for the impossible. No wonder my rival had suggested me.

"Can you do it? I need an answer now," the lady asks impatiently. "They must be ready in time for the King's Ball on Saturday."

"Yes!" I say confidently, amazed at my impulsiveness.

But suppose I fail?

On the other hand, suppose I succeed?

Well, I've got nothing to lose and if I pull it off, I'll go down in history as the first man to have successfully made a pair of glass slippers.

Chapter 11
Dancing Shoes

"Glass slippers? Are you for real? How do you expect me to dance in those? They don't flex, they're likely to shatter and I'll end up with multiple lacerations! What were you thinking? And look at those heels!

"What's that you say? Look in the bag? Oh, there's a pair of flip-flops inside! Well, that's very thoughtful. Yes, I realise you've included them so I can slip them on when my feet start to hurt. I expect that'll be shortly after we arrive, and I step out of my pumpkin carriage.

But wait! Those flip-flops are made of glass too!"

Chapter 12
Escape from the Ball

Balls are boring.

But there was a diversion at this one, and the prince edged nearer to the throng to see what was happening. He arrived as two paramedics carried a beautiful girl out of the hall. Stooping, he picked up what must have been her shoe.

“Slipped,” someone said.

“Knocked herself out,” someone else added.

He looked at the shoe. No wonder she’d slipped; there was no grip on the sole of a glass slipper, and it was coated with pumpkin pulp.

He’d go to the hospital to return her shoe.

What a great excuse to avoid the ball...

Chapter 13
Stuck with Me

*

Prince Charming?

No. There's nothing charming about such a bigoted and obnoxious man. His opinions on the rights of his father's subjects are renowned. He also has an eye for the ladies. That's why I am at this ball, having been glammed up, ready to teach him a lesson. It's amazing what Fairy Godmothers can do with a touch of lippy and a wave of a magic wand.

Here he comes. Lustful eyes and an invitation to dance on his lips. I'm prepared. My palms are smeared with super glue. He's going to be stuck with me until further notice...

Chapter 14
The Seasoned Traveller

*

"I don't know how these youngsters can afford priority boarding," the smartly dressed man said to Mia, nodding at the group of teenagers who were queuing behind them.

"No," she agreed politely, although it didn't cost much extra for priority boarding. Expensive, but hardly exorbitant.

He spent the next ten minutes trying to impress Mia with his knowledge of airlines and travel, and she listened politely, hoping they wouldn't be sitting together.

Finally, the gate opened, and he offered the girl his ticket and passport.

"Scusi, Signor, this flight is for Parma, Italy and your ticket is for Palma, Mallorca..."

Chapter 15
Fashion Critique

*

"Just look at her, dahling! She's got no idea—brown's so drab."

"I know! It's ghastly! And brown with flecks is even worse."

"I must say, you're looking rather splendid today, as usual, dahling!"

"Why, thank you, dear. And so are you. That blue brings out the colour in your eyes and as for that red splash, it's masterful. So becoming!"

The hawk circling overhead suddenly swooped. It didn't notice the small brown, speckled bird which remained camouflaged in the undergrowth, but the two birds with the beautiful plumage were in its sights.

It would take one or the other.

Chapter 16
Enquiring Minds

"What're you s'posed to do with it?" the young boy asked, picking at the thin, brown papery covering.

The older girl nibbled her lower lip. "I think you pull all that paper off," she said.

"It's really difficult. I can't get it all off."

"Try giving it a wash."

The boy held it under the tap. "Do you think that's clean enough?"

"It'll probably do."

"Is it ready now?" he asked.

The girl shrugged.

The boy sank his teeth into it, taking a large bite.

"It's revolting!" He spluttered, spitting out the mouthful and dropping the onion on the floor.

Chapter 17
Silvio's Quest

Silvio flicked his tail, propelling himself through the water, leaving the others behind in a cloud of bubbles. His many siblings swam together, their shiny bodies slipping over each other; so close, they were almost one being. Silvio had been warned not to leave the security of the sardine ball, but he longed to discover the source of the light above them.

"Silvio! Come back!" his siblings called as he sliced upward through the water.

A willing seagull assisted the sardine in his quest to learn what was above the surface. Sadly, Silvio never returned to tell what he'd discovered.

Chapter 18
The Power of Literacy

Librarians' professional whispers. Quiet tiptoed taps. Pages rustling. The murmur of collective knowledge waiting to be discovered.

It's such a privilege to belong to this library.

And one that was denied me in my youth. During my first trip, the librarian told Mother to complete the application form before I could have a library ticket.

To my horror, Mother rushed me away. She could neither read nor write.

Each evening, I crept into the library and hid until an understanding librarian took pity on me, filling in those forms.

That act of kindness unlocked a world of learning and imagination.

Chapter 19
A Box of Ghosts

I have a box of ghosts in my cupboard.

They're all murder victims.

But don't feel sorry for them, for they're all murderers as well. Each has, at one time, wielded a weapon and killed an innocent victim.

Surprisingly, the murderers and the murdered get on extremely well. There's no animosity at all. I suppose they have to live – if 'live' is the correct word for ghosts – in harmony because their roles depend on the roll of the dice.

Now, it's Colonel Mustard stabbing Professor Plum to death in the library with the dagger.

In the next game, who knows?

Chapter 20
Overheard

**

"Well, if I was in charge, I wouldn't bother trying to talk to them. I'd just blast 'em to bits." The lad jabbed his beer can at his mates. "Who needs 'em?"

"Some might be friendly," another one said.

"Nah, destroy 'em all."

Albert took his wife's arm and led her away from the group.

"Did you hear that?" His eyes had narrowed with fury. "That's hate speech. He's encouraging people to blast OAPs to bits."

His wife frowned. "I think you misheard, dear. He didn't say OAPs, he said UAPs. Unidentified Anomalous Phenomena. We used to call them UFOs."

Chapter 21
The Queen's Labour

"The head is visible, your majesty."

No one breathed as she paused to summon sufficient strength for the final push. Unspoken questions hung in the suffocating air of the lying-in chamber. Was the baby alive?

Strong?

A boy?

Her destiny depended on this child. A healthy son would guarantee her status and, if not the king's love, then at least his respect. But if not...

She prayed to the Virgin Mary as she pushed, and the infant slithered, screaming into eager hands.

It was done.

Eyes avoided her gaze and expressions froze.

"Congratulations, your majesty, you have a fine daughter."

Chapter 22
Valentine's Heart

It was dark when Jess awoke. At last, Valentine's Day had arrived.

Excitement rose in her breast, making her heart beat so strongly, she wondered if Roger could feel it vibrate through the mattress. He hadn't slept well. She'd felt him moving restlessly during the night, but his rhythmic breathing indicated he was now asleep.

In ten minutes, they'd have to get up. She offered a silent prayer that Roger's heart operation would be successful. She wouldn't consider the alternative. No, she would be there when he woke up with his new pacemaker and together, they would meet the future.

Chapter 23
The Wishing Pebble

Mark turned the smooth pebble over in the palm of his hand. When Mum had given it to him, it had filled his fist.

Now he was a big boy.

Well, a bigger boy.

Not a big boy, because they didn't cry.

Each night after Dad kissed him and turned his light out, the pain of losing his mother washed over him afresh, and Mark's tears flowed.

"It's a magic pebble," Mum had said, "throw it far into the sea and wish."

Mark closed his eyes, kissed the pebble and whispered, "Come back, Mum."

He hurled it into the waves.

Chapter 24
Make Do and Mend

I don't understand the throwaway generation.

'Make Do and Mend,' was my motto.

"You've broken your doll? Take it to Daddy," Muriel used to say, and I'd get out my well-used tool kit.

But now there is no tool.

It's Muriel who needs mending.

And I've tried. God knows I've tried. But I can't reach her. She no longer recognises me, pushing me away with fear in her eyes as if I'm a stranger.

I'd give anything to repair Muriel's mind and bring back her memory.

My life is one of making do.

But for Muriel, there'll be no mending.

Chapter 25
Tricky

Their courtship had been one of practical jokes, and now Sarah suspected this was another trick.

Peter held out the chocolates "Orange Delight?" His expression was innocent. A whiff of mustard wafted from the box, and she smiled, guessing he'd tampered with her favourite. However, she picked up the Orange Delight and found a diamond ring embedded in the base.

"Marry me?" Peter asked.

"Yes!" She slipped on the ring, popping the Orange Delight into her mouth.

Peter was delighted. He'd fallen for her. She'd fallen for him, and she'd also fallen for his latest prank.

The mustard-laced Orange Delight.

Chapter 26
A Wishing Well

*

The distant hills become one with the night, but at dawn, they emerge from the darkness, silhouetted against the watery light.

I rise, take my water carrier and trek to the well.

One hour later, I am home with my precious cargo.

I set off again.

Three more trips are needed before my family has sufficient water for one day.

Four hours after rising, I set off for school where I will be scolded for tardiness.

I hear that strangers plan to dig a well in my village.

On my walk each morning, I selfishly pray for such a well.

Chapter 27
Good on Him

Imagine a Parisian street in the early 1800s.

Do you see grand horse-drawn carriages? Elegantly dressed people promenading?

Louis Daguerre once took a photograph of the Boulevard du Temple from his studio window, which contains what's thought to be the first photographic image of a human.

An exposure time of four to five minutes meant that carriages and pedestrians moved too fast to be captured. The streets, therefore, appear eerily empty, except for a shoe-shine boy and his customer who remained in position the entire time and have been immortalised.

I wonder if they ever knew they'd achieved such fame.

Chapter 28
The Betrayal

*

Last night, she'd wondered what the other side of fear would look like.

Now she knew.

There was simply resignation and pain. Her wrists and ankles had been rubbed raw by tightly bound ropes, but the agony of her father's betrayal was more acute by far.

It was time.

From the cliff top above her, the king called, "You promised to spare my kingdom in return for a virgin, O Dragon. Behold my daughter…"

The dreadful creature appeared silhouetted against the grey dawn light.

In desperation she cried out, "Wait, Dragon, does the bargain hold if I'm not a virgin?"

Chapter 29
Results

CT scan – check. ECG – check. Blood tests – check.

Then time in the waiting room. Nervous glances at the clock. Hopes raised each time a nurse passes.

Nothing has changed. I'm the same today as I was yesterday or last week, but in a few minutes, I'll have the results of my tests.

Good news?

Bad news?

One in two chance of either.

Finally, the nurse leads us into the consulting room and the consultant rises to shake my hand.

He's smiling. "Good news," he says. "The scans show there has been a spectacular shrinkage in the tumour."

Now I'm smiling.

Chapter 30
Washed Away

No one can hear when I sing in the shower. In the same way, no one can hear when I cry.

The rush of water covers all but the loudest sounds. Tears are washed away from my cheeks before they're fully formed. Once I'm washed and dried, no one would know I've been crying about you, Dad.

Today, six years ago, we held hands for the last time. We were still hand-in-hand when you slipped away from this life and were gone.

My tears may have been washed away, and the sobs drowned but the pain in my heart remains.

Chapter 31
A Lasting Impression

We breathe it in. We breathe it out.

Air.

It surrounds us. It fills us.

And it makes me wonder if it recognises our shape.

Some people believe water has a memory. Why not air?

How much air passed into you and out again while you were alive, Mum?

And is your shape still invisibly impressed upon it somewhere?

If I could find the space where once you'd been, I would wrap my arms around it.

But perhaps, since I'm your daughter, I have already unknowingly embraced that air, and your space in it is now a part of me.

Chapter 32
In One Hundred Years

Our thoughts will be accessible to all and that will be a good thing because although no one can read my mind now, many people believe they can.

How do I know?

Because of reports in the media, both social and traditional, where people state categorically what others are thinking.

Of course, it's tempting to suppose others think in a similar way to ourselves. But that can lead to assumptions about people's opinions, their motives and ultimately their culpability.

One day, our thoughts will be downloaded, examined and stored. Then, perhaps people will stop jumping to conclusions about others' intentions.

Chapter 33
My Parents' Hands

**

Like a book between bookends, my arms extended upwards until my muscles ached, holding their hands. I yearned to wander, but they kept me safe between them.

As a teenager, how embarrassing to have to hold their hands before crossing a road.

When I was old enough to ignore other's opinions, I loved to hold their hands and one day, I realised I was protecting them as they'd protected me.

Finally, I held their hands while their lives ebbed away.

Now all I have is the memory of their hands in mine.

How I wish I'd held them for longer.

Chapter 34
Pure Evil – Pure Love

A human mind first conceived barbed wire. Wicked spikes which snare and rip fabric and skin, entangling men like flies in a web, easy targets for snipers. So simple, yet so diabolical.

Consider flame-throwers and poisonous gas. What manner of man envisaged using those on fellow beings? How can human minds encompass such evil?

Today, I was disentangled from barbed wire in No Man's Land by two stretcher-bearers who risked their lives to save mine. And now I am being looked after by angels in nurses' uniforms.

How can the human mind embrace such contrast?

Pure evil and pure love.

Chapter 35
'Us' and 'Them'

'Us' and 'Them'.

From earliest times, humans formed communities which offered them security and prosperity. For cave dwellers, teamwork may well have been the difference between life and death.

So, the concept of 'Us' was born, but with it came the idea of 'Them'.

'Them', the ones who are not 'Us'.

Today, we still recognise 'Us' and 'Them'.

How many wars have been waged across the globe and throughout time between 'Us' and 'Them'?

In a world where difference is eyed with suspicion, will we ever be able to welcome all members of 'Them' into the group we call 'Us'?

Chapter 36
No Voice

Tipping his head back, he screamed.

Pain, outrage and desperation embodied in that disturbing sound.

No one listened. No one heard, because his shout was lost among so many other clamouring voices.

He wasn't surprised or disappointed. At least he'd had the opportunity to speak.

Suddenly, the crowd fell silent.

Only his voice rang out and once again, he laid bare his agony before all.

No one listened.

No one cared, and he was devastated because he knew conclusively that although he'd been given the opportunity to speak, no one was interested.

He realised he had no voice at all.

Chapter 37

Hot, Bitter Tears

Hot, bitter tears roll down my cheeks.

It's a year since I held your hand, Mum. When I finally had to let it go, it was still warm. That was the last time I would ever touch you.

First, my tears were sad, cold tears of longing and disbelief. Then after that, whenever I thought of you, tears came easily, brimming in my eyes but not falling.

You've never been far from my mind.

Those tears continued throughout the twelve months, but now on October 3rd, the day you slipped away, my tears are hot and bitter with the loss.

Chapter 38
Sleep

Periods of heavy, laboured breathing interspersed with no movement at all, as if you're resting, ready for the next few chest-heaving gasps.

You could almost be fast asleep.

But you're not.

Not yet.

That comes next. A deep and permanent sleep in which there'll be no more struggle.

It was just you and me at the beginning of my life. And now, it's just you and me at the end of yours. You told me how you'd longed for a child for so long and then I arrived. But I've dreaded this time for so long and now it's here.

Chapter 39
Curled Around My Finger

Your hand remains curled around my finger like a baby gripping an adult's finger. A baby reacts by instinct, closing its hand, not knowing what it's gripping.

Do you know my hand is in yours, Mum?

I'll never know. And I wouldn't take my finger away if you didn't – just in case. If there's a chance you're aware I'm here, that's enough.

Your mother was with you when you came into this world. Just you and her.

Your daughter will be with you when you leave. Just you and me.

My finger in your curled hand will be my sign.

Chapter 40
Just You and Me, Mum

Just the two of us at my birth, Mum.

And the two of us at your leaving.

Between those two events, you've always been there for me.

During my childhood, you allowed me room to grow, always ready to catch me when I fell and to wipe away my tears.

Later, separated by distance, you were always there when I needed you.

Our lives have been shared with so many wonderful people during those years – so many loving relationships – but still there is a special bond between you and me which will never be broken, it will last for eternity.

Chapter 41
Extending My Loan

I understand that when something is on loan; it has to be returned eventually. And I know that when you borrow something, you have to treat it with respect as if it were your own, and I've tried to do that. I haven't always got it right, but I've done my best.

Please, I beg you, will you extend the loan?

I know that ultimately you have to take my dad and I'm aware you'll love him more perfectly than me, but if you could let me have him a while longer, I promise to cherish him while I can.

Chapter 42
Journey into the Future

There's thick fog ahead of me along the road and each footstep takes me into the unknown. But I know where I am, and behind me, I can see where I've been. The people I love are with me on my journey, sometimes hidden, but always there.

Until now.

Dad, I know you have to leave, but I don't want to move forward without you. One day, I'll want to look back at all those treasured times with you.

But not now.

It's too painful.

I want to stop and hold you here.

Must we keep moving into the mist?

Chapter 43
Key to the Quiet Room

While I sat in the waiting room outside the Critical Care Unit waiting to be allowed to visit my dad, I looked across the corridor and wondered what lay behind the door opposite.

No one entered, no one left.

On the door was a sign, 'Quiet Room'.

And then before I was ready, I was given the key to the Quiet Room, and I discovered what lay within. A comfortably appointed room filled with pain such as I had never known. A room where my family and I huddled miserably, trying to come to terms with life without my dad.

Chapter 44
10 June 2017

I walked in the garden with my dad today.

I couldn't see him, but I knew he was there by my side because they are both places he loved to be; his garden and next to Mum and me.

I walked the places he would have walked today if he'd still been with us and I remembered his life on the day of his birth. He would have been ninety-one, and we would have spent our time in the garden he loved.

I couldn't see him today.

But I know he saw me.

I know he walked by my side.

Chapter 45
A Shiver of Pain

On patrol in the frozen trench, two soldiers stamp their feet against the frost; fear pumping through their veins.

A shot.

A cry.

Warm, wet dabs of blood and brain on one soldier's cheek. His silent scream is a misty cloud of breath, wreathing his head, while his friend slithers downwards.

Today, the soldier will pay tribute.

He wants to remember everything, but his mind's numb, cutting him off from those memories.

However, each cell of his body has not forgotten.

They will remind him.

As one, they tremble, and the soldier shivers uncontrollably, remembering the cold, fear and shock.

Chapter 46
Earth's Tears

The ground we have taken during the battle can be measured in yards. Each square foot has been soaked in sweat, and each square inch saturated with blood.

The Somme offensive began in July when our optimism almost reached the clear, blue skies.

But now, at the end of November, the clouds are heavy and the frosty air nips at us, hardening the mud in our trenches.

The battle is over. Not because of a decisive victory, but because the Earth has made conditions too hard to continue.

Rain falls like the Earth's tears, washing away our sweat and blood.

Chapter 47
How Could We Have Known?

Success was ours. There was no question.

How could it be otherwise after such careful preparation?

The German trenches had been bombarded for days, and explosives laid beneath them, blowing them sky high.

No one could have survived.

When the whistle blew, we climbed out of our trenches and advanced slowly across No Man's Land.

There was no need to run. After all, we'd already won the battle. Perhaps even the war.

How could we possibly have known the German trenches were untouched?

How could we have foreseen that almost 20,000 of our men would lose their lives that day?

Chapter 48
Scene on the Somme

He hangs broken and twisted on barbed wire coils that crisscross No Man's Land; kilt flapping in the breeze. Transfixed on the metal spikes that have bitten into uniform and flesh, he's an easy target, yet the enemy doesn't fire on him and finish his agony.

Perhaps there are more urgent threats, or perhaps no one wants to waste a bullet on a man who's already trapped in the jaws of death.

The young soldier's head falls back, and his struggles cease.

It's over.

His face, now turned to the French sun, will never feel the soft Scottish rain again.

Chapter 49
One More Year

Exactly one year to go before the madness is over.

Just 365 days.

But as the soldier lights another cigarette in the dawn light, hands cupped to keep the rain from the match, he does not know this. It seems that he has always been here; ankle-deep in mud.

Cold, wet, hungry.

Life before this hell on earth is a distant memory that sometimes appears to belong to someone else.

This is all: mud, shell holes, death, pain, fear.

Only 365 more days to go?

He neither knows nor cares. His prayer is to survive until the day is over.

Chapter 50
I Count

*

It is 100 days since our massive bombardment of the Germans began and 92 days since we went over the top believing this battle on the Somme was ours.

I count everything.

The number of rats per day I see, the number of letters from home I receive each week, the number of pals who've been maimed, the number of those who still lie in No Man's Land.

I can't control this hell; I can only count the consequences.

Now I'm counting the seconds until I go over the top again.

I count everything, yet my life counts for nothing.

Chapter 51
A Gift at Christmas

Tommy and comrades crept out of the trench. Frozen breath hung in the air that crackled with anticipation and hope.

The Germans had promised a Christmas Day truce.

Could they be trusted?

Soldiers in Pickelhauben crunched across the frosty ground, hands high. Then Christmas greetings in German and English filled the air in No Man's Land, where once bullets and shells had screamed.

Fritz approached Tommy, holding out a letter with tear-filled eyes. "Please. In England. You will post this? My wife is English..."

"I will," promised Tommy, shaking hands with the man who, tomorrow, would again be the enemy.

Chapter 52
His First Day on the Somme

He squeezed the lucky rabbit's foot in his pocket. Both hands were needed now.

Gripping the ladder, his palms dripped with sweat and fingers trembled. One foot on the bottom rung, the other ready to push upwards away from the duckboards in the bottom of the muddy trench.

Men on either side waited for the whistle and order to go over the top; silent other than the shuffle of boots, clearing of throats, the whisper of prayers, moans of fear...

Any second now.

He reached into his pocket and stroked the rabbit's foot.

He'd survive the attack. Surely, he would...

Chapter 53
The Other Side of Peace – 1918

The Armistice has been signed. The guns have fallen silent.

The men are on their way home and their women and children await them with relief and joy.

At last, after four appalling years, normal life can be resumed.

But what is 'normal'?

There are too many men who didn't return home.

Too many women and children in mourning, with no grave to visit.

Too many men with physical and mental wounds who will never again know peace.

There is guilt at leaving mates behind, regrets for things done and not done.

For many, life will never be normal again.

Chapter 54
Hooge Crater

A century ago, mines exploded in the Belgian countryside, leaving a deep crater. Men died here in their thousands as it repeatedly changed hands.

Ours.

Theirs.

Ours.

Theirs.

The price of ownership paid in men's lives.

Today, Nature is reclaiming the crater, painting it her signature colours of green and brown. The harsh lines of the concrete bunkers are softened with moss, and a pond lies at the base of the crater. Nearby, discarded shells lie rusting and blue tits live in the barrel of a field gun.

Eventually, Nature will erase all traces of devastation.

LET US NOT FORGET.

Chapter 55
Passchendaele

Whisper it. Passchendaele.

Doesn't it sound like a gentle breath of wind?

But in August 1917, there was nothing gentle about it.

Not when shells were dropping into the quagmire, exploding and sending up columns of muddy, bloody water.

Not when bullets whistled overhead or struck home.

Not when screams filled my ears.

Only dead men were silent. And, of course, the mud.

That sticky, stinking ooze that sucked the unfortunate into its depths.

Not many who slipped into the mire escaped its inexorable pull, and unless eager, desperate hands were able to drag them out.

They are there still.

Chapter 56
My Des Res

I'm keeping out of my mistress's way. She's cross with Master, and the stupid man has acquired that pathetic whine, trying to wriggle his way back into her affections.

Personally, I think he's wasting his time. He came home from the pub drunk again last night. It's not like she hadn't warned him. And now she's furious.

He ought to wait. In fact, it's what I'm going to do – wait outside in my kennel. That's probably a good move because possession is nine-tenths of the law, even for dogs. And despite Mistress's words, the master's not coming into my doghouse.

Chapter 57
The Observer

*

I don't like people.

Large vicious creatures that lash out when I fly by.

Mostly, I don't fly by.

I sit high on their kitchen walls. Watching.

Often, not much goes on.

People come. They go. They eat, read, cook, wash up.

Sometimes they shout and wave arms at each other. Initially, it alarmed me, but now I know there's usually a resolution. Either there are tears and then everything is quiet again or the noise continues. Doors slam. Saucepans clash. Sighs, grunts and tuts.

It’s remarkable what you learn about human behaviour when you’re a fly on the wall.

Chapter 58
I Demand Equality

*

What happened to equality?

It's unbelievable that today, individuals dare pass judgement on others. I pride myself on being as impartial as I can, with no prejudice against anyone.

We come in so many shapes, sizes, colours and patterns and with such a variety of features. I mean, how can you compare a toucan with a peacock? Or a sparrow with a turkey?

You can't, and yet apparently, just because I'm sitting in a bush with my friend, we've been judged, and only deemed to be worth half as much as that bird over there sitting in that man's hand.

Chapter 59
The Wrong Career

*

I should've gone into entertainment like my mum advised.

But when you're young, you always know it all.

Now it's too late to change. I'm not qualified to do anything else.

I do my best, but there's never any appreciation.

Periodically, the stress of my job gets me down. It wouldn't be so bad if I had a friend, but everyone eyes me with suspicion, while actually pretending I'm not there.

No feedback. No thanks. No constructive criticism.

If I had my time again, I'd join the circus. It would be more satisfying than being an Elephant in the Room.

Chapter 60
A Make Over

Laboriously, Marcel climbed up Rapunzel's plait to her tower-top room. His hairdresser's bag was slung over his shoulder. He could have trimmed her ends every six weeks from the ground, but she insisted on a wash and blow-dry. Still, she paid handsomely and appeared to enjoy his visits.

"I'd like it done like this," she said, showing him a photograph. Marcel's professional pride took over. Yes, that style would suit her well. Hours later, she admired her hair in the mirror. "Thank you," she said, tossing the tresses out of the window. "I've always wanted short hair... and a companion."

Chapter 61
A Bid for Freedom

*

Rapunzel studied the complicated drawings the prince had brought to her tower-top prison. "I must admit, I was hoping for a long ladder."

The prince nodded. "Trust me, this is the best option. I've explored all possibilities and the tower's too tall for a ladder. A rope ladder might be a possibility, but it breaches several health and safety regulations."

"So, I climb out of the window into your contraption. Sit on a small mat and then slide to the bottom?"

"Exactly. And afterwards, we'll dismantle it and sell off the design. I'm thinking of calling it a 'Helter Skelter'."

Chapter 62
Training a Champion

*

Tortoise's new fitness coach was a marvel. Each year, in the Tortoise vs Hare Marathon, Tortoise suffered humiliation. He'd given up believing he'd ever win.

But this year, his trainer had worked wonders; Tortoise's body was sleeker, his muscles stronger and his outlook more positive.

She'd bought him a smartwatch with a fitness tracker that measured important parameters: blood oxygenation, pulse, and so on. She'd also downloaded an app to be used in an emergency to boost his performance.

It didn't sound particularly effective, but he trusted her. Now, where was the app? Ah, yes, the one she'd called 'Uber'...

Chapter 63
Tricking a Wizard

"Have you heard? The elf next-door is going to be on Strictly Come Dancing on Saturday."

"What? Pipkin? No! Surely not. He's got two left feet. In fact, he's so clumsy it's like he has three left feet and one of those is on upside down."

"Well, apparently, he tricked a wizard into giving him a pair of magic dancing shoes."

Later...

"Did you see Pipkin on Strictly Come Dancing last night?"

"No! How did he do?"

"He got kicked off."

"But what about the magic shoes?"

"Well, his feet danced well. It was just the rest of his body..."

Chapter 64
Promises, Promises...

*

Father and son Gnome studied the enormous campaign poster. The image of a smiling Gnome with arms outstretched in front of a panorama of the Garden was emblazoned with the words.

VOTE GARBEDGE FOR HEAD GNOME

and underneath in bold type,

WE CAN BE GREAT! WE WILL BE GREAT!

"Impressive, eh, son? He's got my vote. What d'you think?"

"I'm not sure. He hasn't actually said what his policies are."

"It's obvious. His poster says it all. We can be great; we will be great."

"Hmm. But when you get right down to it, Dad, what does that actually mean?"

Chapter 65

Don't Mess with the Skinny Boy

*

John cupped his hands around his mouth and yelled at the skinny boy. "Well, look who it isn't! Did Mummy let you out on your own, then?"

"Don't get mud on your shiny shoes. Mummy might tell you off!" Michael wagged a mocking finger.

"Is that a twig he's waving at us?" John asked.

"Dunno. What you gonna do with that then, Skinny?" Michael shouted.

A flash of lightning streaked from the end of the stick and crackled through the air towards the bullies.

"Ribbett, ribbett?" said John.

"Croak?" replied Michael.

The skinny boy lowered his wand and sauntered off.

Chapter 66
Parents

"I don't want to tell you how to run your life, son," she said, "but the time has come to make some friends, perhaps take up a sport. Get out and enjoy yourself. I know it's scary, but staying in your bedroom talking to an imaginary friend isn't going to help you in the future. A lad of your age shouldn't be so attached to that..." She pointed at the object her son clutched to his chest. "Now, hand it over and I'll get rid of it," she said.

Anxiously, Aladdin backed away; a lamp held tightly against his chest.

Chapter 67
The Princess's Hand

*

"I've told you before, son, stop wasting money on gadgets from that online store. We haven't got enough to fritter away on your weird inventions."

"But Mum! The princess lost a ring in the Royal Meadow and the king's decreed that whoever finds it can have the hand of the Princess. This is my chance to secure my future."

"And you think that metal detector you've built will help you find the ring? That Meadow's huge, and it'll be packed with suitors looking for it."

"Exactly! I'm going to make loads of detectors and sell them. I'll make a fortune."

Chapter 68
A Terrifying Vision

Benny closed his eyes; frozen, immobile with terror as the enormous blobby things approached. Hot air blasted him in rhythmic pulses, and he thought his heart would stop.

There was no escape. The creature held him in a vice-like grip.

Two squashy objects pressed into his damp amphibian skin. Then, thankfully, retreated. But not before the creature emitted a satisfied sigh.

Benny must have passed out with shock, and when he awoke, the world had shrunk, and so had the creature.

"My Prince," it said, wiping its lips with the back of its hand.

Poor Benny's froggy days were over.

Chapter 69
Sibling Rivalry

"Go away!" The princess stamped her foot and glared at her younger brother. "Leave him alone. He's mine."

She shielded the frog balanced on her palm with one hand.

"Isn't it enough you'll be king one day? You take everything I want."

The prince shrugged and, shoving her, he snatched the frog and ran off into the woods, laughing.

He'd soon lose interest, and she'd follow him and steal it back. Then she'd have her prince.

But she was horrified to see two princes, hand-in-hand, stroll out of the clearing. Why did her spoilt brother always get what he wanted?

Chapter 70
Be Sure Your Sins...

**

Geppetto answered his phone. “Pinocchio?”

“Papa! Thank goodness! I’m in trouble! Please, can you help me?”

“Where are you?”

“I’m being held prisoner in a dungeon. The kidnappers are demanding one million Lira, and if you don’t pay by tonight, they’ll kill me.”

“Pinocchio! How many times have I told you to stick to the truth? No one can kill you. You’re made of wood. Stop this nonsense right now.” Geppetto hung up.

Five days later, la Polizia discovered an underground chamber. They arrested a gang of termites after finding an abandoned mobile phone and an enormous pile of sawdust.

Chapter 71
Balancing the Books

The garden gnomes gathered on what had once been the lawn. It was now a jungle.

"The garden lavatories are shut," one of them grumbled.

"No money to pay for someone to look after them," another said. "The library's shut too."

"It's not good enough. Didn't we vote Bartrum in as head Gnome to sort out garden administration?"

"Don't criticise Bartrum. He's a good gnome. I voted for him."

"Perhaps," a passing fairy observed. "If we'd thought about garden services more than cutting taxes before the election, we might still have garden lighting, Troll security patrols and litter-free fairy circles."

Chapter 72
Nobody's Fool

**

Once upon a time, children respected their elders – and the tooth fairy. But not nowadays. Brunhilda shook her head in dismay, mouth pursed in displeasure.

Here was another boy who thought he'd get something for nothing.

As if anyone would mistake a single white Lego brick for a tooth, even in the dark.

Let young Robert have his laugh. She dropped the brick into her tooth pocket and, pulling out her purse, she peeled off two five-pound notes.

Never let it be said a tooth fairy didn't pay the going rate.

One Lego brick for ten pounds of Monopoly money.

Chapter 73
The Elves and the Shoemaker

**

The shoemaker crept out of his hiding place and approached the elf foreman. "Excuse me, my good elf, I'm grateful your elves make shoes for me overnight, but do they have to be so messy? Why don't they put my tools away and clear up any grease on the floor. And why do they need nuts and bolts?"

With hands on hips, the elf foreman replied, "Look mate, how d'you expect an elf to keep a wife and kids on what you pay?"

"Pay? I don't pay you..."

"Exactly, mate. So, we're moonlighting; fixing bicycles to make a living wage."

Chapter 74
To Be a Queen

*

The cries of support are almost lost among jeers and taunts, but they give her little comfort. Once upon a time, the crowds had gathered to praise and cheer her, but people are fickle and easily influenced.

The beads of her rosary move methodically through her fingers, while she offers up silent prayers for her soul and suddenly, at an unseen signal, the crowd falls silent.

It is time.

Gripping the rosary tightly, she flings her arms sideways to indicate her readiness. Her exposed neck feels the disturbance of the air as the axe blade slices downwards.

The crowd gasps.

Chapter 75
Janus's Dilemma

*

I detest New Year, even though I'm the god of beginnings and endings.

It's most disconcerting looking in front and behind simultaneously. People always want to know what you can see when you look forward.

But no one's interested in what I'm viewing as I peer backwards into the year just gone. They already know what happened.

No, all they are interested in is the future.

A Roman god can easily fall out of favour, especially the bearer of bad news. Whatever I see, I nod wisely, making apologetic sounds while smiling enigmatically.

Let them interpret that as they wish!

Chapter 76
Noisy Neighbours

*

"Good evening, officer, I wish to complain about my next-door neighbour."

"What's the problem, madam?"

"Noise. It's been like that for three days now. I can't sleep at night with all that singing. There's a huge choir, all dressed in white."

"I see..."

"I don't suppose you do, officer. I've never seen or heard anything like it. And as for the mess..."

"Mess?"

"Those ruffians who turned up yesterday bought a flock of sheep. And as for the three turbaned gentlemen who arrived on camels… Honestly, the next-door neighbour's got no business allowing a baby to stay in his stable."

Chapter 77
World Cup Memories of 1966

*

I'm not a football fan, but there's one match in 1966 I remember clearly.

I need say no more, for it's gone down in English history.

I was on holiday with my parents and while Mum read by the swimming pool, Dad and I made our way to the hotel's single television with everyone else to watch the game.

When those words 'They think it's all over... It is now!' were spoken, Dad and I looked at each other in amazement.

Enormous smiles on our faces, we crept out of the silent room, leaving the German supporters to their sorrow.

Chapter 78
In the Tidy Silence of Loneliness

*

In forty-eight years, she'd never got used to bits on the carpet immediately after she'd cleaned, snoring from his side of the bed, empty toilet roll holders, drawers and doors left open…

Even after so long, she'd never got used to those aggravations. Mostly, she'd rolled her eyes or ground her teeth and occasionally, she'd erupted, to be accused of unreasonableness.

But now he was gone, and she longed for the sound of noisy breathing from his side of the bed and the mess which meant he was there.

What she wouldn't give to have the chaos of him, back.

Chapter 79
Wise Words

**

The manager surveyed the copywriter over the top of his steepled fingers.

"Frankly, Charles, I'm disappointed," he said.

"Oh?" Charles sat upright, a worried frown on his brow.

"Yes, I suspect you didn't write this at all." The manager waved a sheaf of papers in the air. "In fact, I'm guessing you got Artificial Intelligence to write it."

Charles blushed. "How did you know?"

"It's nothing like your normal style. Actually, it's better than your usual work."

"Then, you like it?"

"I don't know, Charles. If you can't be bothered to write it. I can't be bothered to read it."

Chapter 80
That Takes the Biscuit...

If 9% of people in the UK hide biscuits in their sock drawer, it suggests biscuit-snatching is rife.

If only biscuits could talk, they could shout for help. That would prevent biscuit crumbs in socks and drawers.

Although, what might biscuits say at the moment of dunking or nibbling? Would they give in gracefully, or be outraged?

An angry biscuit? Who'd want to risk it?

Suppose they kept chattering?

The only biscuit I'd like to listen to would be the one sold at auction for £15,000. It had been rescued from the Titanic. What a story that biscuit could tell...

Chapter 81
Date Biscuits

"How'd the big date go?"

Babs sadly shook her head. "It was a disaster. He was so inconsiderate. I won't be seeing him again."

"But why? He looked so promising on the dating app. He was handsome and well-dressed. And he had the same taste as you in so many things. What went wrong?"

"He spectacularly failed my dating test."

"Your dating test?"

"Yes, I offered him my tin of assorted biscuits, and he made straight for the chocolate coconut crumblies. And then he took three! How could I possibly fall for a man who scoffed all my favourite biscuits?"

Chapter 82
Don't Give up the Day Job

**

Recently, on my travels in France, I saw a strange black bonnet with a cape attached on a mannequin outside a shop. It looked as though it was a hat for someone who didn't want to be seen.

I wondered if it was possible to invent a completely new fashion. Surely it was.

I decided to start at the bottom. Shoes with socks combined? No, that's certainly been done already.

Okay, shoes with socks and trousers combined. And attach a jacket to that. And to finish it off, what about a hood?

Hmm, I seem to have invented the onesy.

Chapter 83
My Dream

**

All I want is a chance.

A new beginning. A fresh start.

I want to draw a line under what's gone before. To bury those memories, to stifle the screams that fill my imagination and forget the horrors I've witnessed.

I'm asking for one little break.

An opportunity to start my life in a new country, away from the terrors I have experienced.

I climb into the inflatable boat – no lifejacket, no seat, no one to care if I should disappear. I hunker down and stare at the choppy waves that lap the horizon.

Please, just give me a chance.

Chapter 84
Anyone for Tennis?

Wimbledon. Ugh.

"Play." Plock... plock... plock...

"OUT."

I've got tennis to look forward to for the next fortnight. There'll be no escape. Nothing sensible on television or radio. The newspapers will be full of it.

"New balls please." Plock... plock... plock... plock...

"OUT."

I ought to turn the television off and do something productive. Perhaps clean the kitchen... No, I'll just watch the end of this game.

Plock... plock...

Oof. I didn’t think she’d get that one. What a good shot. I might keep watching to see if she wins. And this bowl of strawberries is certainly sweetening things up.

Chapter 85
Not an Average Girl

It wasn't as if Mrs Connolly wanted to be in charge of Careers. She was happy teaching history, but the head had insisted.

The whole fiasco was getting on her nerves. In the good old days, boys had wanted to be train drivers and girls, nurses. Now, under the influence of Instagram and Tik-Tok, most students aspire to being famous.

"Ah, Mavis, come in. Have you any ideas about a career?"

Mrs Connolly braced herself. Mavis always wanted to be different. She'd probably want to be a popstar and influencer.

"Oh, yes, Miss. I'm going to be a Flower Fairy."

Chapter 86
Robert

**

The case was baffling. A man had died in his bed. Nothing unusual about that. No suicide note, although police received a letter from someone called Robert, claiming to have killed him.

A nutter? Perhaps. But Robert had described the bedroom with its peaceful green wallpaper and furnishings. He'd obviously been there.

"Green décor?" Alfie, the rookie detective, asked at the briefing. "Like in Napolean's bedroom?"

Everyone rolled their eyes.

"That's how Napolean died," Alfie said.

He'd been right. The green pigment in the wallpaper contained copper arsenite, which gave off toxic fumes.

And guess the name of the decorator...

Chapter 87
The Party in the Gallery

The thief crept into the art gallery, listening for the party. He knew the characters in each painting gathered together in one frame each night. Switching the lights on would freeze them in place. After all, they wouldn't want to be seen hopping from one frame to another. They'd wait until it was dark and then creep back to their own frame, ready for the day.

"Now!"

The thief's accomplice turned the lights on.

Grabbing the frame with all the characters in it – men on horseback, cherubs, women with vases, dogs… the thief smiled, knowing that painting would be priceless.

Chapter 88
Enduring Torture

It's torture – pure and simple.

Gripping the arms of the chair so tightly, my knuckles turn white, I grit my teeth, bracing myself for the next assault.

A brief pause and then it hits me again, the sound slicing through my eardrums and drilling into my brain.

Ironically, lack of practice has turned her into a master torturer.

Not that she intends harm.

Far from it.

Her role as my tormentor is not her idea.

Her parents have insisted she take violin lessons.

And I, the unfortunate wretch who was engaged as her music tutor, must silently endure the pain.

Chapter 89
The Extra

You won't find me in the spotlight on the world's stage.

I'm one of the crowd.

Sometimes a member of the chorus.

Or simply waiting in the wings to walk on unseen in an insignificant role.

It's easy to overlook me. Simple to ignore me.

But if everyone who makes up the crowd or chorus in this production that we call Life, is removed, the stage would be bare.

There'd still be scenery, costumes and principal characters bathed in pools of light. The performance would still go on. But without the 'unimportant' cast members, wouldn't the whole production be one-dimensional?

Chapter 90
Silence on Remembrance Day

Daily, we are bombarded with noise and commotion that demands our attention. There is little time to think.

But if we were to consider the wars in our past and spend time reflecting on the conflicts in our present, would we be able to avoid future bloodshed or strife? Would we be able to make the world safer for our children?

Today, we remember the lives of those who died to give us a future.

We honour them with our silence. We are still. We are quiet.

Indeed, what is there to say?

Words are hollow sounds; inadequate, imperfect, distracting.

Chapter 91
Humankind vs Tardigrade

One day, Earth's conditions may become too hostile for human survival.

When deserts are scorched, land is flooded and temperatures plummet or soar, making life impossible… the Tardigrade may become the dominant lifeform on Earth.

Tardigrade? An alien species or science fiction?

Neither.

These microscopic creatures have inhabited Earth since Cambrian times. They're ugly, wrinkled, eight-legged creatures which withstand desiccation, boiling, freezing, crushing and radiation – yet still survive.

Humankind, with its intelligence, empathy and creativity, seems unwilling or unable to respond to the threat of climate change. Our negligence may result in our destruction.

Then, Tardigrades will inherit our world.

Chapter 92
Colour Coordinated

A field of cauliflowers is a beautiful sight. Row upon row of yellow heads waiting to be picked.

Stop! Wait!

Yellow?

What a disaster!

No one'll buy yellow cauliflowers unless they're an heirloom variety. Supermarkets require pristine white heads, believing their customers prefer perfection.

I'll only eat cauliflower if it's smothered in cheese sauce, and by then, I can't tell what colour it had been when it was picked. I wonder how many others would know or care either.

How irresponsible and wasteful to leave perfectly good fields of food to rot, simply because they don't match the colour chart.

Chapter 93
The Small Print

What's the difference between "I'm sorry" and "I apologise"?

Is there a difference?

I'd never given it much thought. But now, I think there's something more important to consider, and that's the words that come after "I'm sorry" or "I apologise".

I didn't realise until a few years ago when someone told me he was sorry I was hurt.

Surely anyone is sorry when they see someone in pain – not because they caused it, but because they empathise.

I took his words as an apology until I realised he hadn't taken responsibility for his actions; simply said he was sorry.

Chapter 94
The World on Loan

*

The librarian looked in horror as the woman returned a broken, torn book.

“Pages are missing,” he said indignantly.

The woman smiled. “Don’t worry, they came out after I’d read the book, so I know what happens.”

“I’m going to have to charge you for the damage,” the librarian said.

The woman shrugged.

In the future, will the owner of the world – God, your interpretation of God or perhaps our descendants – look at the broken, torn environment and point out the damage we caused?

Will we shrug and reply, “Don’t worry, we used up what we wanted of the world.”?

Chapter 95
My Heroes

If you've ever waited for medical results, you may have been told they're still at the lab.

'The lab'. As if it's a wayward person who's deliberately delaying your results.

Years ago, I worked in a microbiology lab. We poured agar plates containing different nutrients suitable for common bacteria. Several times a day, swabs, sputum, stools, blood were delivered, logged and cultured on the appropriate agar plate.

Then, we advised doctors which antibiotics were appropriate for their patients.

Scientists run labs.

They still do, working out of sight. Possibly risking infection themselves.

I sincerely salute those silent and invisible heroes.

Chapter 96
The Art of Smiling

When many celebrities are photographed, they lift the corners of their mouths into an upward curve. They part their lips slightly, showing perfect teeth. Then they freeze. At first sight, it appears they're smiling – but they're not. They pull that face, so their eyes don't close to slits and the skin around them doesn't crinkle.

Until I knew that and even tried it, I'd assumed the most important part of a smile involved the mouth. But it doesn't. A true smile comes from the eyes.

Don't believe me?

Remember lockdown when everyone wore masks? Couldn't you tell who was smiling?

Chapter 97
Familiarity Breeds...

Familiarity Breeds Contempt – or Content?

Essex, – the county of spectacular mountains, dramatic countryside, and beautiful beaches?

No. Not at all. Essex is pleasant, mediocre, ordinary. Some might even say dull.

I grew up in a town in Essex that in 1965 became part of Greater London, so I may have forfeited the right to be an 'Essex Girl'. However, I moved deeper into Essex as I grew up and have lived nowhere else.

I was educated here. I met the love of my life and married here.

So, is Essex outstanding? No, but it's the place that made me what I am.

It's my home.

Chapter 98
Alien Invasion

People of Earth, you foolishly believe you can thwart our plans for your destruction.

Think again.

For a time you managed to impede our progress but your tactics and weapons are failing. Ironically despite your superior intelligence, you have been the ones to help us in our bid for supremacy and we have mutated until we have outsmarted you.

Where will we attack?

Our attack has already begun.

Do not appeal to our hearts, we have none.

We kill to survive.

Either you die or we die.

But it will be you, once we gain resistance to the latest antibiotics.

Chapter 99
Relaxing Massage Chairs

While Relaxing Massage Chairs are indeed chairs, they are not relaxing nor do they massage. Admittedly, this has more to do with my lack of height than design flaws in the chairs. During a recent encounter, I lay with my head touching the top of the body-shaped cavity, while my feet finished where my calves should have been.

The rollers which should have gently pummelled my muscles were not aligned with the correct parts of my anatomy. Consequently, all my bony parts were squeezed and kneaded, as if being pounded by relentless golf balls.

Such deceitful contraptions should be banned.

Chapter 100
The Giants of Gold Beach

**

Last week I stood with Giants.

Not fairytale giants.

These were silent silhouettes standing vigil on the hill above a D-Day landing beach. The figures of soldiers, sailors and airmen honoured 1,475 British men who died eighty years ago on 06 June, attempting to liberate France.

They landed sea-sick and afraid yet determined to bring sanity to a world gone mad.

Among the silhouettes were those of two women – nurses who died rescuing seventy-five men from a sinking hospital ship. And in the woods were figures of men, women and children belonging to the French resistance.

We will remember them.

Also by Dawn Knox

The Great War – 100 Stories of 100 Words Honouring Those Who Lived and Died 100 Years Ago

One hundred short stories of ordinary men and women caught up in the extraordinary events of the Great War – a time of bloodshed, horror and heartache. One hundred stories, each told in exactly one hundred words, written one hundred years after they might have taken place. Life between the years of 1914 and 1918 presented a challenge for those fighting on the Front, as well as for those who were left at home—regardless of where that home might have been. These stories are an attempt to glimpse into the world of everyday people who were dealing with tragedies and life-changing events on such a scale that it was unprecedented in human history. In many of the stories, there is no mention of nationality, in a deliberate attempt to blur the lines between winners and losers, and to focus on the shared tragedies. This is a tribute to those who endured the Great War and its legacy, as well as a wish that future generations will forge such strong links of friendship that mankind will never again embark on such a destructive journey and will commit to peace between all nations.

Order from Amazon:

Paperback: ISBN: 1532961596 eBook: ASIN: B01FFRN7FW

A Cottage in Plotlands

The Heart of Plotlands Saga – Book One

London's East End to the Essex countryside - will a Plotlands cottage bring Joanna happiness or heartache?

1930 – Eighteen-year-old Joanna Marshall arrives in Dunton Plotlands friendless and alone. When her dream to live independently is cruelly shattered, her neighbours step in. Plotlanders look after their own. But they can't help Joanna when she falls in love with Ben Richardson – a man who is her social superior… and her boss.

Can Joanna and Ben find a place where rigid social rules will allow them to love?

Order from Amazon:

Paperback: ISBN: 9798378843756 eBook: ASIN: B0C4Y9VZY9

Also **A Folly in Plotlands**, **A Canary Girl in Plotlands, A Reunion in Plotlands** and **A Rose in Plotlands**

The Duchess of Sydney

The Lady Amelia Saga – Book One

Betrayed by her family and convicted of a crime she did not commit, Georgiana is sent halfway around the world to the penal colony of Sydney, New South Wales. Aboard the transport ship, the Lady Amelia, Lieutenant Francis Brooks, the ship's agent becomes her protector, taking her as his "sea-wife" – not because he has any interest in her but because he has been tasked with the duty.

Despite their mutual distrust, the attraction between them grows. But life has not played fair with Georgiana. She is bound by family secrets and lies. Will she ever be free again – free to be herself and free to love?

Order from Amazon:

Paperback: ISBN: 9798814373588 eBook: ASIN: B09Z8LN4G9 Audiobook: ASIN: B0C86LG3Y4

Also, **The Finding of Eden, The Other Place, The Dolphin's Kiss,** and **The Wooden Tokens**

The Post Box Topper Chronicles

Book Four in the Chronicles Chronicles Series

A boring post box. Five knitters. Can one woman convert a post box into a work of artistic genius?

Vera Twinge is a natural leader. As chairperson of the newly formed Creaping Bottom Post Box Topper Society, she's determined to make a splash in the village's High Road with a stunning new post box topper for each month. But she's constantly obstructed by an unscrupulous journalist, an insulted hairdresser and a possible mass murderer. Urging her society members on to create more ingenious toppers, Vera refuses to be defeated. But with negative reports in the local newspaper, a revenge haircut and the threat of alien invasion, Vera wonders if she is up to the task.

Will Vera and her post box topper society expose the strange happenings in Creaping Bottom and keep their beloved post box an object of beauty?

Order from Amazon:

Or from the Bridgetown Cafe Online Bookshop: Paperback: ISBN: 191576212X eBook: ASIN: B0D9HCYB7T

About the author

Dawn would be thrilled if you would consider leaving a review for this book on Amazon and Goodreads, thank you.

If you'd like to know more about her books, you can find out by joining the Readers Club on her website: https://dawnknox.com

About the Author

Dawn spent much of her childhood making up stories filled with romance, drama and excitement. She loved fairy tales, although if she cast herself as a character, she'd more likely have played the part of the Court Jester than the Princess. She didn't recognise it at the time, but she was searching for the emotional depth in the stories she read. It wasn't enough to be told the Prince loved the Princess, she wanted to know how he felt and to see him declare his love. She wanted to see the wedding. And so, she'd furnish her stories with those details.

Nowadays, she hopes to write books that will engage readers' passions. From poignant stories set during the First World War to the zany antics of the inhabitants of the fictitious town of Basilwade; and from historical romances, to the fantasy adventures of a group of anthropomorphic animals led by a chicken with delusions of grandeur, she explores the richness and depth of human emotion.

A book by Dawn will offer laughter or tears – or anything in between, but if she touches your soul, she'll consider her job well done.

If you'd like to keep in touch, please join the Readers Club on her blog and receive a welcome gift, containing a collection of short stories, exclusive material and two photo-stories. She often updates the welcome gift with new material.

Following Dawn:

Blog: https://dawnknox.com

Amazon Author Central: Dawn Knox https://mybook.to/DawnKnox

Facebook:

X: _https://twitter.com/SunriseCalls

Instragram: https://www.instagram.com/sunrisecalls/

YouTube:

Printed in Great Britain
by Amazon

57912805R00081